THIS CANDLEWICK BOOK BELONGS TO:

_____

_____

_____

_____

To Eve Barsham
with love
G. W.

For my mates
Tini and Richard
D. P.

Text copyright © 1994 by Gina Wilson
Illustrations copyright © 1994 by David Parkins

First U.S. paperback edition 1997

The Library of Congress has cataloged the hardcover edition as follows:

Wilson, Gina.
Prowlpuss / by Gina Wilson ; illustrated by David Parkins.—
1st U.S. ed.
Summary: Prowlpuss, a king-size cat with one ear and one eye,
stalks the night but comes home at dawn, forsaken by one love
but with another awaiting his return.
ISBN 1-56402-483-0 (hardcover)
[1. Cats—Fiction. 2. Stories in rhyme.]
I. Parkins, David, ill. II. Title.
PZ8.3.W697Pr   1995
[E]—dc20   94-1598

ISBN 0-7636-0287-6 (paperback)

2 4 6 8 10 9 7 5 3 1

Printed in Hong Kong

This book was typeset in Parkins.
The pictures were done in watercolor.

Candlewick Press
2067 Massachusetts Avenue
Cambridge, Massachusetts 02140

PROWLPUSS

Gina Wilson

illustrated by

David Parkins

CANDLEWICK PRESS
CAMBRIDGE, MASSACHUSETTS

Prowlpuss
is cunning
and wily
and sly,

A king-size cat
with one ear
and one eye.

He's not a
sit-by-the-fire-
and-purr cat,
A look-at-my-
exquisite-fur cat.
No, he's not!

He's rough and
gruff and very
very tough.

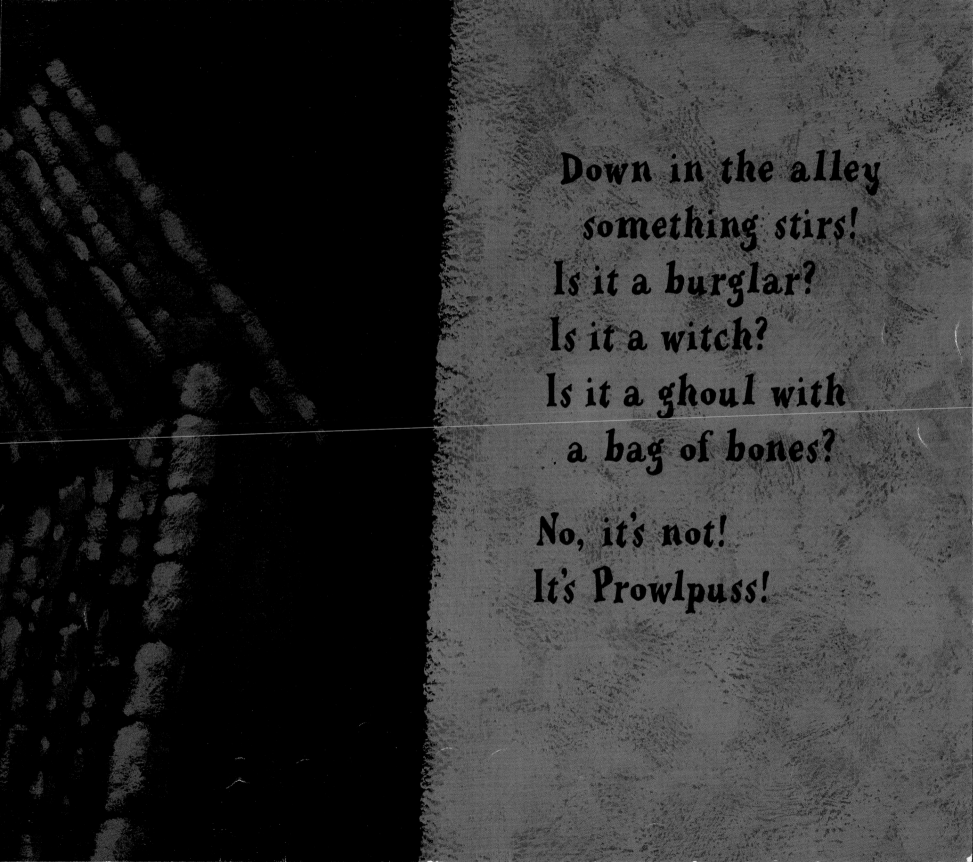

Down in the alley
something stirs!
Is it a burglar?
Is it a witch?
Is it a ghoul with
a bag of bones?

No, it's not!
It's Prowlpuss!

He's not a lap cat,
a cuddle-up-
for-a-chat cat.
No, he's not!
He's not a sit-in-
the-window-
and-stare cat.
He's an *I-was-
there!* cat.

Watch out!
Prowlpuss about!

He's not a stay-at-home cat.
 No, he's not!
He's not a sit-on-the-mat-
 and-lick-yourself-down cat.
He's an out-on-the-town cat,
A racer, a chaser,
A "You're a disgrace"-er!
A "Don't show your face"-er!
He's not a throat-soft-as-silk cat,
A saucer-of-milk cat. No, he's not!
He's a fat cat, a rat cat,
A "What on earth was that?" cat.

So what's it all for –
All the razzle and dazzle,
The crash, bang, wallop,
The yowling, the howling,
The "Give us a break!"
"Don't keep us awake!"
"Beat it!" "Clear off!"
        "Get lost!" "Scram!"
"Good riddance!"?

Who is he wooing
With his hullabalooing
Night after night?   AHA!

High in a tree
  at the alley's end,
Right at the top
  so no one
  can get her
Or fret her
  or pet her,
Lives one little cat—

A tiny-white-star cat,
A twinkle-afar cat.

In the moonlight
she dances,
Like snowflakes
on branches,
She spins
and she whirls.

But not for long!
In a flash she's gone!

Now Prowlpuss
will sing for her—
What he would
bring for her!
Oh, how he
longs for her!
Love of his life!

If she'd only
come down...
But she won't!
No, she won't!

Back through
the alley
slinks Prowlpuss
at dawn,
Love-lost and lorn.

And old
Nellie Smith
in her deep
feather bed
Lifts her head.

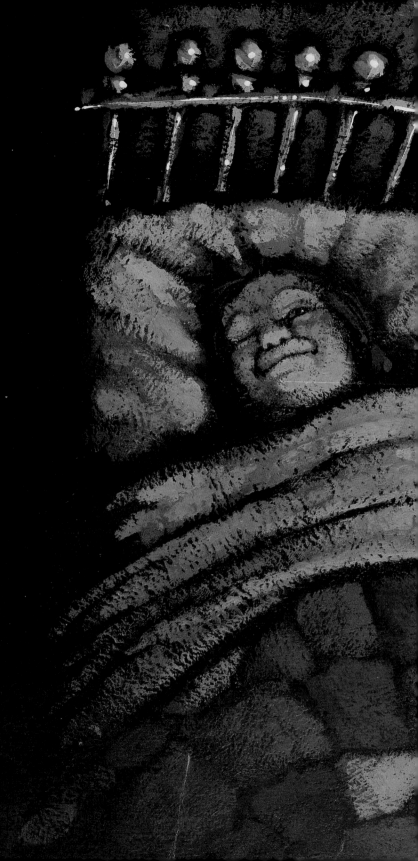

"That's Prowly come home!
That's my jowly Prowly!
My sweet Prowly-wowly!
My sleep-all-the-day cat,
My let-the-mice-play cat,
My what-did-you-say? cat,
My soft and dozy,
Oh-so-cosy,
Tickle-my-toes-y,
Stroke-my-nose-y

Prowlpuss."

Gina Wilson teaches creative writing and has written several novels for young adults, as well as three picture books and a book of poetry for children. She notes that the simple stories of picture books allow the writer "to express significant truths about life. *Prowlpuss,* for example, is about that yearning one always has for the unattainable."

David Parkins employed a technique new to his work to create the illustrations for *Prowlpuss.* "I used watercolors as if they were oil paints, mixing in lighter paints, rather than water, with the darker colors. The process allowed me to make whole areas of the paintings disappear into black, the way light does in an alleyway at night." David Parkins is also the illustrator of *No Problem* and *Tick-Tock* by Eileen Brown, the Sophie books by Dick King-Smith, *Aunt Nancy and Old Man Trouble* by Phyllis Root, and *God's Story,* a retelling of the Old Testament, by Jan Mark.